The White Stallion

by ELIZABETH SHUB

pictures by RACHEL ISADORA

Greenwillow Books
New York

Library of Congress Cataloging in Publication Data

Shub, Elizabeth.
The white stallion.
(Greenwillow read-alone books)
Summary: Carried away from her wagon train in
Texas in 1845 by the old mare she is riding, a
little girl is befriended by a white stallion.
[1. Horses—Fiction.   2. West (U.S.)—Fiction]
I. Isadora, Rachel, ill.
II. Title. III. Series.
PZ7.S5592Wh [E] 81-20308
ISBN 0-688-01210-8   AACR2
ISBN 0-688-01211 -6 (lib. bdg.)

T 4344

For J. B.
—E. S.

For Maureen and Jim
—R. I.

This is a true story, Gretchen.
My grandmother Gretchen,
your great-great-grandmother,
told it to me.
She was as young as you are
when it happened.
She was as old as I am
when I heard it from her.

It was 1845. Three families
were on their way West.
They planned to settle there.
They traveled in covered wagons.
Each wagon was drawn
by four horses.
Conestoga wagons they were called.

Gretchen and her family
were in the last wagon.
Mother and Father sat
on the driver's seat.
The children were inside
with the household goods.

Bedding, blankets, pots and pans,
a table, chairs, a dresser
took up most of the space.
There was not much room left
for Trudy, John, Billy, and Gretchen.
Gretchen was the youngest.

Behind the wagon
walked Anna, their old mare.
She was not tied to the wagon
but followed faithfully.
She carried two sacks
of corn meal on her back.

It was hot in the noonday sun.

The children were cranky and bored.

The wagon cover shaded them,

but little air came in

through the openings

at front and back.

John kicked Billy.
Billy pushed him,
and he bumped Gretchen.
Trudy, the oldest,
who was trying to read,
scolded them.

Their quarrel was interrupted
by Father's voice.
"Quick, everybody, look out!
There's a herd of mustangs."
The children clambered
to the back of the wagon.

In the distance
they could see the wild horses.
The horses galloped swiftly
and, in minutes, were out of sight.

"Look at Anna," John said.

The old mare stood rigid.

She had turned her head

toward the mustangs.

Her usually floppy ears

were lifted high.

The wagon

had moved some distance

before Anna trotted after it.

15

It was hotter than ever inside.

"Father," Gretchen called,

"may I ride on Anna for a while?"

Father stopped the wagon

and came to the back.

He lifted Gretchen onto the mare.

The meal sacks

made a comfortable seat.

He tied her securely

so that she would not fall off.

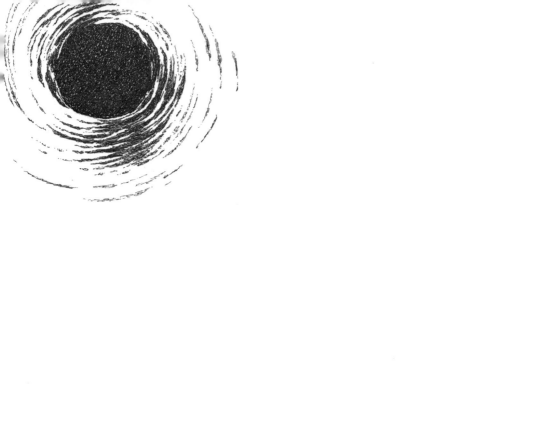

As they moved on,
Gretchen fell asleep,
lulled by the warmth
of the sun.

They were following
a trail in Texas
along the Guadalupe River.

The rear wheel
of the first wagon
hit a boulder,
and the axle broke.
The whole train stopped.

Anna strayed away,

with Gretchen sleeping

on her back.

No one noticed.

The travelers made camp.

Children were sent for firewood

and for water from the river.

The women prepared food.

It was not until the axle
had been fixed
and they were ready to eat
that Gretchen and Anna
were missed.

The men tried to follow
the mare's tracks
but soon lost them.
It was getting dark.
There was nothing to do
but remain where they were.
They would search again
at the first sign of light.

Faithful Anna, they thought,
would return.
She probably had discovered
a rich patch of mesquite grass.
She would come back
when she had eaten
all she wanted.

Gretchen awoke to the sound
of lapping.
Anna was drinking noisily
from a stream.
A short distance away
stood a herd
of ten or twelve wild horses.
They were brownish in color.
Some had darker brown stripes
down their backs.
Others had dark markings
on their legs.
They were mares.

After Anna had finished drinking,
she moved toward them.
And they walked forward
as if to greet her.
When they came close,
they neighed and nickered.

They crossed necks with Anna,
nuzzled her and rubbed against her.
They were so friendly
that Gretchen was not afraid.
And she did not realize
that Anna had wandered
far from the wagon train.

Suddenly the horses
began to nibble
at the sacks on Anna's back.

They had smelled the corn meal.

In their eagerness

they nipped Gretchen's legs.

Gretchen screamed.

She tried to move out of the way.

She tried to loosen the ropes

that tied her.

But she could not reach the knots.

Terrified, Gretchen screamed

and screamed.

Out of nowhere

a great white stallion appeared.

He pranced and whinnied.

He swished his long white tail.

He stood on his hind legs,

his white mane flying.

The mares moved quickly
out of his way.
The white stallion
came up to Anna.
He carefully bit through the ropes
that tied Gretchen.

Then, gently, he took hold
of the back of her dress
with his teeth.
He lifted her to the ground.

He seemed to motion to the mares
with his head,
and then he galloped away.
The mares followed at once.
Anna followed them.

Gretchen was left alone.

She did not know what to do.
"Father will find me soon,"
she said out loud
to comfort herself.
She was hungry,
but there was nothing to eat.
She walked to the stream
and drank some water.
Then she sat down
on a rock to wait.

She waited and waited,
but there was no sign
of Father.
And no sign of Anna.
Shadows began to fall.
The sun went down.
The dark came.
"Anna!" Gretchen called.
"Anna! Anna! Anna!"

There was no answering sound.

She heard a coyote howl.

She heard the rustling

of leaves and

the call of redbirds.

Gretchen began to cry.

She made a place for herself
on some dry leaves
near a tree trunk.
She curled up against it,
and cried and cried
until she fell asleep.

Morning light woke Gretchen.

The stream sparkled

in the sunlight.

Gretchen washed her face

and drank the clear water.

She looked for Anna.
She called her name,
but Anna did not come.
Gretchen was so hungry
she chewed some sweet grass.
But it had a nasty taste,
and she spat it out.

She sat on her rock
near the stream.
She looked
at the red bite marks
on her legs
and began to cry again.

A squirrel came by.

It looked at her

in such a funny way

that she stopped crying.

She walked along the stream.

She knew she must not go far.

"If you are lost,"

Mother had warned,

"stay where you are.

That will make it easier

to find you."

Gretchen walked back

to her rock.

It was afternoon when she heard
the sound of hooves.
A moment later Anna
ambled up to the stream.
The sacks of meal were gone.
The old mare drank greedily.
Gretchen hugged and kissed her.
She patted her back.
Anna would find her way
back to the wagon train.

She tried to climb on Anna's back,
but even without the sacks
the mare was too high.

There was a fallen tree
not far away.
Gretchen wanted to use it
as a step.
She tugged at Anna,
but Anna would not move.
Gretchen pulled and shoved.
She begged and pleaded.
Anna stood firm.

Now again

the white stallion appeared.

Again he lifted Gretchen

by the back of her dress.

He sat her on Anna's back.

He nuzzled and pushed

the old mare.

Anna began to walk.

The white stallion

walked close behind her

for a few paces.

Then, as if to say goodbye,

he stood on his hind legs,

whinnied, and galloped away.

Gretchen always believed
the white stallion had told Anna
to take her back
to the wagon train.
For that is what Anna did.

Your great-great-grandmother Gretchen

bore the scars of the wild mare bites

for the rest of her life.

I know because

when she told me the story,

she pulled down her stockings.

And I saw them.